SCIENCE COURT
TO SERVE AND OBSERVE™

The Case of the Big Drip

Adapted by Craig Strasshofer

Based on an original TV episode written and created by Tom Snyder, Bill Braudis, and David Dockterman

Illustrated by Bob Thibeault and Kristine Koob

Troll

1

DRIP, DROP, PLOP

I. M. Richman was a very important businessman, and he looked the part with his large mustache and expensive three-piece suit. He could have taken a taxi to work, or had his chauffeur drive him, but he preferred to take the subway. He liked to think of himself as being in touch with the common folk. One day as he stood on the subway platform reading the newspaper while waiting for the train, he noticed a girl staring at him. He didn't know it, but her name was Micaela.

"What are you staring at, kid?" Mr. Richman asked.

4

The girl just kept staring. Suddenly a drop of water fell from above and landed on the ground in a puddle forming around Mr. Richman's feet. He was so busy being important that he didn't even notice.

"You're standing in a big puddle of water," Micaela said.

"Run along," Mr. Richman answered. "Shoo, shoo, little person! Good-bye!"

"You're still in a puddle," said Micaela.

The girl's gaze began to get on Mr. Richman's nerves, and he decided it would be best to move. "Fine, then," he said. "I'll move away from you! Don't follow me." Mr. Richman took one step, slipped in the puddle of water, and tumbled to the floor. "Whoaaaaaaa!" he screamed.

Micaela just stared at Mr. Richman sitting there in the puddle. "Now you're sitting in a puddle," she said.

Lying flat on his back in the puddle, he

looked up to see that the water appeared to be dripping from some pipes that ran along the ceiling high above him. Just at that moment, another drop fell and hit him plop in the eye. Right then and there he decided to find out who was responsible and to make them pay for the damage he had suffered (although, in truth, he was not badly hurt at all). "Hey!" he shouted loudly. "I'm going to find out who is responsible for those leaky pipes."

Mr. Richman started to get up.

"You're still . . . " Micaela began.

As Mr. Richman got to his feet, he slipped and landed in the puddle once again.

"Waaaaa!" cried Mr. Richman.

"Oh, never mind," said Micaela.

2

PIP AND HER PIPES

The next day, Pip Peterson, owner of Pip Peterson's Pipe and Plumbing Company, sat at the desk in her large office, surrounded by beautifully displayed examples of the pipes and other high-quality plumbing supplies manufactured by her company. Unfortunately, she was upset. Her hand trembled as she pushed the buttons on her telephone, which was custom-made in the shape of a bathtub. She was calling Alison Krempel, Science Court's best defense lawyer. Pip needed help.

"Yes, hello, Ms. Krempel?" Pip said into

the phone. "I need your help. They say my pipes are leaking, but they can't be. I mean, people are slipping in puddles, probably even as we speak. But it can't be my pipes."

"Calm down," Alison Krempel said on the other end of the phone. "First, I'll need to know who you are."

"Oh, yes, of course. I'm sorry. My name is Pip Peterson. I own Pip Peterson's Pipe and Plumbing."

"Makes sense," said Alison.

"Now, I'm telling you, Ms. Krempel," Pip went on, "my company does good work. Our pipes don't leak."

"Then what is the big problem?" Alison asked.

"People are saying our pipes leak," Pip explained. "I'm being called to appear in Science Court."

"Did you get a call from—?" Alison began.

9

Pip finished the sentence for her. "Yes. A man named Doug Savage called me. He sounded very serious."

"Oh, really?" said Alison. "What did he say?"

"Well," Pip told the lawyer nervously, "he's representing someone who slipped on the subway platform. I heard you were the best Science Court lawyer around. Will you help me, please?"

"Ms. Peterson, you sound like a nice person," said Alison. "I'd love to help you."

THE OLD SOFTY

The day of the big trial finally arrived. As usual, Stenographer Fred had come to work early. He was sitting on the courthouse steps eating a delicious, although not-so-nutritious, breakfast of doughnuts and coffee. Just as Fred stuffed a big piece of doughnut into his mouth, Science Court reporter Jen Betters showed up.

"Hi, Fred," Jen said.

"Mmmph," Fred replied. He washed the doughnut down with a huge gulp of coffee. "I mean, hi, Jen. Big case today, huh?"

"Yep. Looks like it," Jen agreed.

"Yeah . . . this is the kind of case a stenographer dreams about," said Fred.

"Really? Why's that?" Jen asked.

"Well, it's got everything," Fred told her enthusiastically. "It's got pipes . . . it's got, um, water, and plumbing . . ."

Jen looked at her watch. "Yeah, right. It does sound exciting. Well, time to file my report. You coming?"

"I am psyched," Fred rambled on. "This is going to be a great case. This is going to be like one of those ones . . ."

Fred kept talking as Jen went up the steps and into the courthouse.

Before long they were sitting in Science Court waiting for Judge Stone to begin the proceedings. I. M. Richman caused a stir when he entered the courtroom with a pillow tied to his rear and took a seat next to his lawyer, Doug Savage. Alison Krempel was already there with her client, Pip Peterson.

With just moments to go before the trial, Jen Betters began her broadcast. "Hi. I'm Jen Betters reporting live from Science Court, where science is the law and scientific thinking rules. Judge Stone is about to start the trial right now—"

"Hey, Jen. How are you?" Doug Savage broke in.

"Uh, I'm on the air right now, Doug," Jen replied.

"Oh, sorry," said Doug.

Jen turned back to face the camera. "That's attorney Doug Savage, folks," she explained. "I can tell you that he's got his hands full with this case today."

"Really?" Doug asked with a worried frown on his face.

Judge Stone entered the room, took her seat at the judge's bench, and banged her gavel. "Order," she said. "Order in the court. Today we . . . um . . ." She took a careful look around at the people in the courtroom. "Where's Stenographer Fred?" she asked no one in particular.

At that moment, Stenographer Fred came running into the room. "Here . . . here I am, Your Honor," he said, gasping for breath. "I just . . . I had to wash my hands. They were all sticky. No more doughnuts, Fred." Fred had a habit of talking to himself. He hurried to his desk and said, "All rise."

"They already rose," said Judge Stone.

"All be seated," said Fred.

"They are all seated," said Judge Stone. Then she went on, "Okay, today Mr. Savage charges that Pip Peterson of Pip Peterson's Pipe and Plumbing sells leaky pipes . . . down by the seashore."

At this, Alison Krempel spoke up. "Your Honor, I don't remember seeing anything in the complaint about the seashore."

"Yeah, I was kidding," Judge Stone said

with a little laugh. "Okay. There's also an alleged injury to a Mr. I. M. Richman. Is he here?"

Mr. Richman stood up, and everyone snickered at the pillow tied to his bottom.

Judge Stone banged her gavel again. "Order, order," she insisted. "People, there's a time for laughing and there's a time for being serious. And the time for laughing was when I made that joke about the seashore, but you all missed it. Mr. Richman, you can sit down now."

"Ooh. Oooh. Ow," said Mr. Richman as he eased his fanny onto the chair. This only made the audience in the courtroom laugh even more.

"Mr. Richman is claiming that the pipes made by Pip Peterson's Pipe and Plumbing are leaking," said Judge Stone. "Stenographer Fred, are you ready?"

"Oh, yes, I am!" replied Fred. But he was

so anxious to show how ready he was that he knocked over a cup of water that was sitting on top of his desk. "Oops! Your Honor, I just spilled my glass of water. Should I get a . . . something?"

"You can get a something later," Judge Stone said impatiently. "Ms. Krempel, your opening statement, please."

"Yes. Thank you, Judge Stone. Ladies and gentlemen of the jury," Alison began, "we intend to prove that Pip Peterson's pipes do not leak."

"Mr. Savage, your opening statement, please," said Judge Stone.

"Thank you, Your Honor." Doug rose. "We intend to prove that Pip Peterson's pipes are leaking. And because they're leaking, a frail, lonely, pathetic old man—"

"Excuse me," Mr. Richman broke in, "I am not frail."

"Don't worry," Doug whispered to him

theatrically, "I'm just playing it up."

Mr. Richman nodded. "Oh . . . right. Sorry to interrupt."

"So, where was I?" Doug went on. "A smelly—"

"Oh, dear," said Mr. Richman.

"—lonely—" said Doug.

"Harrumph," Mr. Richman muttered.

"—rickety—"

"Doug, I'm right here," Mr. Richman exclaimed. "I'm in the room!"

"Shhh!" Doug shushed. "And because of those leaky pipes, this man slipped and hurt his . . . uh, well, wait till you see the photos. Thank you."

"Okay, then. Let's do it," Judge Stone ordered. "Mr. Savage, call your first witness."

"Thank you, thank you," Doug replied. Then, in a panic, he turned to Mr. Richman and mumbled, "My first witness is late."

"Uh, late?" asked Mr. Richman.

"I think I told him the wrong time. See, the clock in my bedroom is fifteen minutes fast. The clock in my—"

"I . . . I—" Mr. Richman began.

"—kitchen is—" Doug continued.

"I get the idea," said Mr. Richman.

"—ten minutes behind," Doug finished.

"Maybe I should I take the stand now?" Mr. Richman suggested.

"That's not necessary," said Doug. "I'm going to stall until my witness shows up."

"Is that a good idea?" Mr. Richman wondered.

"Just watch me," Doug replied. Then he turned to Judge Stone and said, as smoothly as he possibly could, "Your Honor, before I get started, could you tell me when you first got interested in the law? Maybe some dates, law school stories, or something along those lines? I'll be sitting right here."

"Should I put my hand over your

mouth?" Mr. Richman asked as he put his hand over Doug's mouth.

Doug tried to reply, "It's not necessary, really. I . . . " But his voice came out all muffled.

"Mr. Savage, where is your witness?" asked Judge Stone.

Doug pulled Mr. Richman's hand away from his mouth. "Uh . . . unfortunately, he's late," Doug admitted.

"Okay, then," the judge told him, "call your next witness."

"Right," said Doug.

4

ROOMFUL OF RAIN

Mr. Richman was the next witness. He got up and walked to the witness stand with the pillow still tied to his rear for all the spectators to see. They laughed and giggled a little more, but they were starting to get used to it. With Mr. Richman settled on the witness stand, Doug began his questioning.

"Mr. Richman, please tell the courtroom what happened that fateful morning when you were on the subway platform and you slipped in a puddle of water and fell."

"Well," said Mr. Richman, "I . . . slipped in a puddle of water and fell."

"Oh, you fell!" Doug exclaimed.

"Yes," said Mr. Richman.

"And how did that water get there?" Doug asked.

"It dripped from pipes installed by Pip Peterson," Mr. Richman declared.

"No more questions, Your Honor," said Doug. "Your witness, Ms. Krempel."

Alison Krempel approached the witness. "Mr. Richman," she began, "did you actually see water dripping from the pipes onto the floor?"

"Yes, I most certainly did," Mr. Richman replied. "And I have a witness who could testify on my behalf if she would just stop laughing."

If you listened closely, you could hear the faint sound of laughter coming from somewhere in the courtroom. It was Micaela, sitting in the front row of the gallery right behind Doug Savage.

"I am not a joke," Mr. Richman said. "I am a man!"

Again the sound of laughter could be heard.

"Thanks, but that won't be necessary," Alison said. "I believe you. I have no more questions."

"So, Mr. Savage, do you have another witness?" Judge Stone asked.

"Uh, not on me, Judge," Doug replied,

searching through his pockets. "Any minute now, though."

"Ms. Krempel, how about you?" asked Judge Stone.

"Yes, thank you, Your Honor," Alison answered. She called the first witness for the defense, Maria Hernandez, TV's weekend weather woman. Alison asked Maria to tell the court her occupation.

"I'm a meteorologist," Maria said.

"And as a meteorologist, you . . ."

"I report the weekend weather on Channel 23," Maria explained.

"Yes, of course," said Alison. "So, Maria, as a meteorologist you study the weather and atmosphere?"

"Yes," Maria responded.

"So you must know about water and air?" Alison asked.

"Of course," said Maria. "Water and air are the two main ingredients of weather."

"Now, you've had a chance to inspect the pipes in question, right?" Alison asked.

"Objection!" Doug objected loudly. "Ms. Hernandez is a meteorologist. She's not a plumber."

"I didn't say she was a plumber," Alison replied.

"Oh." Doug paused. "In that case, Your Honor, I withdraw my objection, and for the record, I just say 'hmm.'"

"'Mmmm?'" Fred asked.

"No. 'Hmm,'" Doug said, "like 'hum.'"

"Oh, okay." Fred nodded.

"Thank you, Mr. Savage," said Judge Stone.

"You bet," Doug answered with a smile.

"So," Alison continued, repeating her question, "you saw the pipes?"

"Yes," said Maria.

"In your professional opinion, was the water dripping from the pipes because of a leak?" Alison asked the TV weather woman.

"No," Maria answered.

"Well, how else did the water get there?" Doug broke in.

"Mr. Savage, no more outbursts," Judge Stone warned.

Doug apologized. "Sorry, I snapped."

"May I explain, Your Honor?" Maria asked.

"Yes," Judge Stone answered. Then she turned to Doug and said, "See how polite she is?"

"Mmmm," Doug mumbled. "Hmm-hmm-hmm-hmm."

"Mr. Savage," Maria requested, "would you touch the outside of the glass of ice water that's in front of you?"

Doug touched the glass and said, "Uh, it's wet."

"Yes that's correct," Alison confirmed. "The air formed water on the outside of the glass, just like it's forming water on the outside of the pipes."

"Objection, Your Honor," Doug said. "The water on the glass came from inside the glass."

"No, it did not," Alison stated firmly. "The water came from the air."

Doug Savage thought this was the most ridiculous thing he'd ever heard. "The air?" he scoffed. "Oh, you mean it was just raining inside the courtroom? Funny, I didn't see a rain cloud in here."

"Ms. Hernandez isn't talking about rain, Mr. Savage," Alison explained. "She's talking about water in the air."

"That's right—" Maria began.

But Doug interrupted again. "Water just roaming around in the air? That's a good one, Ms. Krempel. Water roaming around in the air. Hmph. I don't think so."

"Your Honor, please . . ." Alison said as

she pointed at Doug and made a face.

"Okay, that's enough you two," Judge Stone ordered, banging her gavel. "We'll take a little, short recess . . . and when I say 'recess' I mean, you know, the jungle gym . . . and let everyone cool off."

"Judge Stone says everybody take five," Stenographer Fred announced. "I'm not just a stenographer. I'm the bailiff, too."

Jen Betters turned to the camera. "Is air full of water?" she asked. "Doug Savage says it isn't. We'll be back in a few minutes to find out."

5

CONDENSATION SENSATION

As soon as everyone had finished playing on the jungle gym, they filed back into the courtroom, where Jen Betters continued her broadcast. "Welcome back," she said. "We're waiting for Judge Stone to return to find out if there really is water in the air."

Right behind Jen, TV viewers could see, Doug Savage stood waving into the camera.

A moment later, Fred announced, "The Honorable Judge Stone is back. Everybody stop talking."

"Thank you, Fred," Judge Stone said. "Is there water in the air? I believe that's where we left off. Ms. Krempel, please continue."

"Thank you, Judge," Alison said. "Ms. Hernandez, where does the water on the outside of the glass come from?"

"It comes from the air through a process known as condensation," Maria answered.

"Condemnation?" Doug asked.

"Condensation," Maria corrected. "Let me show you. We'll take two identical empty glasses and leave one on the table and put the other one in the refrigerator."

"Now what?" Alison asked.

"We wait ten minutes, then compare the two," said Maria.

The people in the courtroom fidgeted and whispered among themselves while they waited for ten minutes to pass. Then Maria took out the glass that was in the refrigerator and set it next to the other one. "What do you see?" she asked.

"Well," Alison observed, "nothing seems

to be happening to the glass that was sitting on the table, but the glass that was in the fridge is getting wet on the outside."

"Here," Maria went on, "let me show you." She produced a chart illustrating a human skeleton. "Oops, sorry," she said with a giggle, "wrong chart."

Quickly she pulled out another chart, the right one this time. "You see," she explained, "air is made up of different gases. One of the gases is water vapor. There's water vapor in all air."

"See," Alison said to Doug.

"But when the air is humid—" Maria continued.

"Like it is in here," Alison interrupted.

"Yes, like in here," Maria agreed. "Then there's even more water vapor in the air. And when water vapor is cooled—"

HUMIDITY IS THE AMOUNT OF WATER VAPOR IN THE AIR. WHEN THERE IS MORE WATER VAPOR IN THE AIR, IT IS MORE HUMID. LESS WATER VAPOR MEANS IT IS LESS HUMID.

MORE HUMID

LESS HUMID

"Like when it touches a cold glass or a cold pipe," Alison added. Then she realized how rude she was being. "I am so sorry," she apologized. "Go ahead."

"When water vapor is cooled," Maria began again, "the particles that make up the vapor condense into drops of water."

"Let's say Stenographer Fred is in his car," Alison said.

"Where am I going?" Stenographer Fred asked.

"It doesn't matter," Alison replied.

"This is crazy," Fred muttered.

"Anyway," Alison went on, "his windshield fogs up because the air in his car is warmer than the windshield glass, so the water vapor condenses against the glass."

"That's correct," said Maria. "That's why only the cold-water pipes are covered with water. They're the ones that make the water condense."

"In other words," Alison concluded in a confident tone, "the pipes are not leaking."

"That's right," Maria concurred.

"Wait a minute," said Doug. "How does the water get into the air in the first place?"

"The water gets into the air through a process known as evaporation," explained Maria.

"That's what it's called when liquid water turns into water vapor?" Doug asked.

"Yes," said Maria.

"That's evaporation," Alison confirmed.

Doug was trying to get things straight in his mind. "So when the water vapor turns back into liquid water, is that what you call condensation?"

"Yes, very good," praised Maria.

That made Doug feel proud.

Maria continued giving her testimony. "Water evaporates, condenses, and falls back to earth, only to evaporate again. We call this process the water cycle."

"Excuse me," Fred asked. "Am I still in my car?"

"No, Fred," Judge Stone said patiently. "You're back here with us."

"Okay," said Fred.

Just then, Jen leaned over to Doug and whispered, "Your witness just showed up."

"Your Honor," Doug piped up, "I'd like to call my other witness to the stand now."

"Sure," said Judge Stone.

38

Jen turned to face the camera and in a hushed tone asked, "Does Doug Savage have a trick up his sleeve? Or does this water cycle thing have him all washed up?"

"Hey!" Doug said with a hurt expression on his face. But he pulled himself together and carried on. "I'd like to call Paul Plummer to the stand."

Paul Plummer took the witness stand, and Doug began his careful questioning. "Mr. Plummer . . ."

"Yeah," Paul Plummer replied.

"Please clearly state your last name and occupation," Doug said.

"Plummer and plumber, in that order," the witness answered.

"In other words," Doug clarified, "your name is Plummer, and you also happen to be a plumber."

"Not in other words," Paul Plummer said. "Those are the words."

"Right." Doug smiled. "Boy, I bet you get kidded a lot about the Plummer-plumber thing, huh?"

"No," Paul Plummer answered seriously.

Doug couldn't help but chuckle at his own joke. "Anyway, Mr. Plummer—"

"Why don't you call me Paul?" Paul Plummer suggested.

"Uhh . . . no," said Doug.

"All right," said Paul.

"Paul," Doug went on, "if there was a hole in a pipe, and clear water was in that pipe, what color would the water be that leaked out of that pipe?"

"Clear," Paul replied.

"Your witness, Ms. Krempel," Doug said with satisfaction.

"No questions," Alison called out.

"That was amazing, Mr. Savage," Judge Stone commented.

Paul Plummer stepped down from the

witness stand without uttering another word.

"If it pleases the court," Doug said, "I'd like to perform a little demonstration."

Everyone on the jury thought it was a good idea. They liked demonstrations.

"Yeah, I'm pleased."

"That'll please me."

"Sure, that's pleasing."

"Very pleasant."

"Thank you," said Doug. With that, he produced a burner and an elaborate model of pipes and tubes. "I've created a model of the evaporation-condensation system supposedly happening at the subway station. Will Maria Hernandez please retake the stand?"

Maria returned to the witness stand.

"Now then," Doug continued, "at this end we have a beaker of water on top of a burner. I add some food coloring to make it red so we can follow it. Next, I heat the water. Right, Ms. Hernandez?"

"That's right," Maria acknowledged with a nod. "You are adding energy to the particles that make up the water, so they move faster. As they move faster, the water particles move farther apart—that creates the steam. The steam then disappears when it all turns into water vapor."

"So now we can follow the steam up this tube here and over onto this pipe here, which is made by Pip Peterson and is filled with cold water," Doug explained as he traced the path of the steam moving steadily through the tube. "Ms. Krempel, why don't you tell us what is happening?"

"The far end of the pipe appears to be dripping water into the cup," Alison said.

"And what color is the dripping water?" Doug asked.

"Clear," Alison mumbled.

A big smile appeared on Doug's face. "I'm sorry, Ms. Krempel, what you just said wasn't very clear. Would you say it again a little more clearly?"

"Clear! Clear!" Alison exclaimed. "The water's not red, it's clear."

"And what color is the water that is evaporating?" Doug asked.

"Red," said Alison.

"Exactly!" Doug declared triumphantly. "Red water evaporates, yet it's clear water that's dripping from the pipe. It's not the same water. Therefore, the pipe must be leaking."

"Your Honor, I object," Alison objected. "Mr. Savage is completely misinterpreting the experiment."

"Misinterpreting? Why, I've never been so insulted in my life," said Doug.

"Sure you have," Alison replied. "What about the time you . . ."

"Shhh!" Doug shushed.

Suddenly Fred spoke up. "Your Honor,

all this talk of water is making me, you know . . . I think I have to go to the men's room."

"Can't you wait one minute?" Judge Stone asked.

"No, Your Honor, please, please . . ." Fred whined.

"Me, too," pleaded Alison.

"Well . . ." The judge hesitated. "Can't you just wait a few minutes while I—"

"I don't think so," Alison said.

Judge Stone let out a deep sigh. "Anyone else?"

The members of the jury all spoke at once.

"Yeah."

"We gotta go."

"Right now."

"Hurry up."

"Oh, okay," Judge Stone relented. "We'll take a short break while I review Mr. Savage's dripping experiment." She banged her gavel firmly on the bench and declared a recess.

"Okay," Fred yelled, "everybody, go, go, go!"

As the room emptied, Jen Betters turned to face the camera. "Wow! There's a lot going on. We'll come back to Science Court in a moment to find out what's happening."

6

PROFESSOR PARSONS PIPES UP

Everyone felt a lot better after the recess. As soon as things had settled down, Judge Stone appeared from her chambers and took her place at the bench.

"Everybody get up," Fred ordered. "The judge is back."

"Thank you, Fred," said Judge Stone.

"All be seated," Fred said.

"Thank you," repeated the judge. "Now, Mr. Savage, that was quite an impressive demonstration."

Doug blushed just a little. "Aw, shucks," he said modestly.

"However," Judge Stone continued, "I have to agree with Ms. Krempel."

Doug's modesty immediately turned to disappointment. "What?"

"Your conclusion was incorrect," said the judge.

"You're kidding!" Doug exclaimed.

"The heated, colored water evaporated, and the water vapor traveled up the tube," Judge Stone went on. "As the vapor cooled, it condensed and dripped down into the cup."

"Right," Doug agreed. "But it was clear water, not red. So it must have come directly from the pipe."

"No," Judge Stone corrected him. "If you look in the bottom of the original water container, I think you'll see something interesting."

Doug held the beaker up close to his face and peered inside. "Hey, what's all this red stuff on the bottom?" he asked.

"Water evaporates," the judge explained, "food coloring does not. And neither does anything else that might be in the water."

"But, but, but . . ." stammered Doug.

"Think about what happens when you leave nice fresh Play-Doh out overnight," said Judge Stone. "I'm not saying do it, I'm saying think about it."

"Judge, I never leave my Play-Doh out overnight," Doug objected.

"Why not?" Judge Stone asked.

"Because it gets ruined," Doug said. Then he turned to Micaela and whispered, "Can you believe these people?"

"I think she wants to know why it gets ruined," Micaela whispered back.

"Oh, right," Doug murmured to her. He turned to Judge Stone and said, "It gets all hard and crumbly, and then you can't make little elephants and skyscrapers and poodles and . . ."

"Exactly," said Judge Stone, "because all of the water evaporates out of it."

"Well . . . okay," Doug agreed. "But just because Ms. Krempel has shown that water vapor can condense on the outside of cold pipes doesn't mean that that's the only thing happening here."

"Oh, come on!" Alison sighed.

"He's right," Judge Stone said.

Alison couldn't believe her ears. "What!" she gasped.

Doug couldn't believe his ears either. "I am?" he asked.

"We still don't know for sure if the pipes are leaking or not," said the judge.

"Okay, then," Alison declared, bouncing back from her surprise. "I call Professor Parsons to the stand."

Professor Parsons was a highly educated person and a regular expert witness in Science Court. He quickly took the witness stand and waved to the crowd with a cheerful, "Hello, everybody."

"Professor Parsons," Alison started off, "what do you do?"

"I am an overqualified science teacher at the local university," Professor Parsons replied, chuckling to himself.

"Professor," Alison went on, "please tell us what you have there." She pointed to a pipe and a beaker of water resting on a table next to the witness stand.

"This is a way to test if any water is escaping from inside these pipes," said the professor. "It's really quite simple."

"And how does it work?" Alison asked.

"Well," Professor Parsons explained, "here I have a section of Pip Peterson's pipes, identical to those that are dripping."

"Identical, Mr. Savage," repeated Alison.

"Yeah, yeah, yeah," Doug answered grumpily.

"One end of the pipe is sealed," the professor continued. "I fill the pipe with cold water and seal the other end, like so. Isn't that a wonderful procedure?"

"Now what?" Alison inquired.

"Well, now I measure the mass of the pipe," said Professor Parsons.

Alison crossed the room and took the scales of justice down from the courtroom wall. "Here you go," she offered.

"Uh, thank you, but that won't do," said the professor. He produced an enormous and complicated-looking measuring device. "Beautiful, isn't it? I put the pipe on this measuring device and see that it has a mass of six hundred grams."

"Objection," Doug objected.

"Now what?" Judge Stone asked.

"I don't know what six hundred grams is," Doug said.

"Think of a paper clip. That's about one

gram," Micaela suggested helpfully.

Doug leaned over to Jen and remarked, "Wow. She's good."

"Okay, what now?" Alison asked the professor.

"Wait," Professor Parsons replied.

"What?" asked Alison.

"We wait," said the professor.

"Oh, right." Alison nodded.

"Of course we wait," the professor said. "We can talk among ourselves, though," he added with a chuckle.

They waited.

"Anyway," the professor suddenly piped up, "notice how the pipe is getting wet?"

"Yes," said Alison. "So how long do we wait?"

"As long as you want," Professor Parsons replied.

"I don't want to wait any longer," said Alison.

"Okay. Touchy!" The professor raised his eyebrows. "Now we measure the mass of the pipe again and see that it actually has more mass."

"Why is that, Professor?" Alison asked.

"Because we're also measuring the mass of the added condensed water on the outside of the pipe," answered the professor.

"Well," said Doug, "you should wipe off the water and then measure the pipe's mass."

"Why, thank you very much, young man," Professor Parsons commented with a laugh as he wiped the water off the outside of the pipe. "I will."

"Anybody could figure that out," Doug whispered to Jen.

"Now the mass of the pipe should be the same as when we started this experiment," the professor explained.

"Unless it's leaking," Doug added.

"Unless it's leaking," Professor Parsons

agreed as he put the dry pipe on the scale. "Uh, let's see. Let me check the, uh . . . everybody having fun? All righty, then. The mass is exactly the same. It's not leaking at all, even though the pipe was covered with water."

"So clearly the water did not come from inside the pipe," said Alison.

"No," the professor concluded. "No, it did not."

"Thank you, Professor Parsons," Alison said. "No more questions."

"Questions, Mr. Savage?" Judge Stone asked.

"Eeww," Doug moaned, thinking hard. "Actually, I have a question I'd like to ask Ms. Krempel."

"Yes?" Alison said.

"Am I correct to assume that you are basing your entire case on this water cycle thing?" Doug asked.

"Yes, Mr. Savage," Alison replied. "It's common science."

"But there are inconsistencies," Doug said, pointing to where Fred had spilled his water earlier in the trial. "Look. The water Stenographer Fred spilled on the floor earlier today has disappeared."

"Hey, it's gone," Fred said. He leaned over to get a closer look and spilled another cup of water.

"But Judge Stone's glass of water has been here all day and it hasn't evaporated," Doug went on. "Are we to believe that some water evaporates and some water doesn't? If the water doesn't feel like evaporating, it doesn't have to? Is that what you're saying, Ms. Krempel?"

"I can explain the water in Judge Stone's glass," Micaela said.

"Raise your hand," Judge Stone insisted.

Micaela raised her hand.

"Ahhh, yes, you," Judge Stone said, as if noticing Micaela for the first time.

"It's really simple," Micaela began.

"Oh, I suppose you're going to tell me it's evaporating, but just very slowly," Doug scoffed.

"Actually, it is," Micaela replied.

"Hey, I was being sarcastic," Doug said.

"Mr. Savage," Alison explained, "only the little bit of water on the surface that touches the air can evaporate." Then she turned to Micaela. "Am I right?" she asked.

"Yes, ma'am," said Micaela.

"So if I . . ." Alison grabbed a glass of water and threw the water at the blackboard. Some of it splashed onto Fred, who was sitting nearby.

"Hey! I'm typing here," Fred said.

"She did it! She did it!" Doug shouted, hoping to get Alison in trouble.

". . . if I spread the same amount of

water out so that it's all touching the air, it will evaporate quickly," Alison concluded. "See?"

"Your Honor, Ms. Krempel is being flippant," Doug complained. "I move for a mistrial."

"I'll bet you do," said Judge Stone.

"Your Honor, I'm ready now for closing arguments," Alison told her.

Doug slowly leaned over to Jen. "Any suggestions?" he asked.

"Give up," Jen replied.

"How about you?" he asked Micaela.

"Nope," Micaela said with a shrug.

"Oh, well," Doug sighed.

7

ALISON RAPS THINGS UP

Jen looked thoughtfully into the camera. "Well, it's come down to closing arguments, and it doesn't look good for Science Court attorney Doug Savage."

"Hey!" said Doug. "It's not that bad . . . maybe."

"Mr. Savage, are you ready to make your closing argument?" Judge Stone asked.

"Ladies and gentlemen of the jury, let's not forget the victim in this case," Doug began. "That guy sitting right there, uh, Mr. . . . uh, what was his name? He slipped in a puddle . . . Richman, that's it. He slipped in a puddle that was a direct result of pipes installed by Pip Peterson."

Meanwhile, Professor Parsons was still on the witness stand. "Excuse me," he said. "Could I, uh, could I leave now? I've got a class to get to."

"Oh, yes," the judge replied, "I'm sorry."

"Thank you, Judge," Professor Parsons said with yet another happy chuckle. "I had a terrific time. All around. Really."

The professor hurried out of the room, chuckling as he went, and Doug went on with his closing argument, such as it was. "Uh . . . so, in conclusion . . . Pip Peterson's guilty. Thank you very much."

"I think I missed something," Alison commented.

"Okay, Ms. Krempel," Judge Stone said. "I guess you're up."

Doug started to giggle. He turned to Jen and whispered, "It sounded like she said

'Europe,' didn't it? 'You're up,' 'Europe'? Get it? That's—"

"Uh . . ." Jen said, trying to ignore him.

"—funny," Doug finished.

"Yeah," Jen said.

Then Alison rose and proceeded with her closing remarks. "Thank you very much, Your Honor. Members of the jury," she said firmly. "Pip Peterson's pipes don't leak. They're actually victims of the water cycle. We all know about evaporation and condensation. You know, you climb out of a pool, soaking wet, then the sun beats down. Heat speeds up every water molecule. Then some molecules escape, evaporate, and hide out till it's cool. Then they slow back down, condense again, and rain into the pool."

Alison's speech had a rhythm like a rap song. The members of the jury started tapping their feet, and before long they were dancing all over and joining right in.

"Evaporation!" one juror yelled.

"Condensation!" hollered another.

"It keeps on going round!"

"That's why it's called a water cycle!"

"Get down!"

"Ain't it funky now!"

Judge Stone banged her gavel. "Order. Order, please."

"Thank you," said Alison, returning to her seat.

"No, thank *you,* Ms. Krempel," Judge Stone replied.

"Your Honor, can I have a do-over?" Doug asked.

"No," Judge Stone said. "Members of the jury, you've heard the evidence. Now you must decide whether Pip Peterson is guilty of . . . leaky pipes. Court is recessed until the jury reaches a verdict." She banged her gavel again and hurried out of the room.

Jen Betters looked the camera straight in

the eye. "And there goes the jury," she said with great excitement. "It doesn't look good for Doug Savage."

"Hey!" said Doug.

"But stranger things have happened," Jen continued. Suddenly she put her hand up to the tiny receiver in her ear and listened intently. "Oh, wait a minute. I just got word that the jurors have reached a verdict."

"Already?" Doug exclaimed. "That fast? They just left."

Jen went on with her report. "We'll be back in a moment to hear their decision."

"But that's good, right?" Doug rambled on. "Don't you think it's good when they decide so quickly?"

THE JURY GETS TO THE BOTTOM OF THINGS

The members of the jury filed back into the room and took their seats in the jury box. Judge Stone didn't waste any time in getting things moving.

"Members of the jury," she said, "have you reached a verdict?"

Everyone on the jury started talking at once, making a horrible jumble of sound.

"Yeah, we did."

"I think so."

"Sure."

"Very pleasant."

"Can we go now?"

"Uh, just the foreperson, please," Judge Stone broke in.

"Me?" the foreperson asked.

"Yes, you," said Judge Stone.

"Now?" the foreperson asked.

"Yep," said Judge Stone, glancing at her watch.

The foreperson cleared her throat. "We, the jury, find Pip Peterson and her pipes . . . innocent! Not guilty!"

"Thank you, jury," said Judge Stone.

"Oh, wait, one more thing," added the foreperson. "We are sorry that Mr. Richman fell on his . . . uh . . . bu . . . bu . . . fanny. Can I say 'fanny' in court?"

"Absolutely!" Judge Stone told her. "I insist upon it. You can say 'fanny,' 'derrière,' 'buttocks,' 'bottom,' . . ."

"Oh, thank goodness!" The foreperson chuckled. Some other jury members giggled, too. "But condensation is everywhere, and we feel he should be more careful."

"Very good," Judge Stone acknowledged.

"Oh, hold on, one more thing," said the foreperson.

"Uh huh," replied Judge Stone, sighing.

"We think it would be a nice gesture if Pip Peterson looked into the condensation problem to see if maybe she could use different pipe materials or some sort of insulation," the foreperson suggested.

"Okay, that—" said Judge Stone, raising her gavel.

"And one more thing," the foreperson interrupted again.

"Oh, come on," Judge Stone groaned.

"We recommend that Doug Savage never, ever wear that shirt and those pants together again," the foreperson said. All the other members of the jury nodded their heads in agreement.

"Good." Judge Stone said quickly. "I agree with the jury's decision. Science Court is now adjourned."

"What? Science Court is a germ?" asked Stenographer Fred.

Judge Stone gave her gavel a nice, hard bang.

"Everybody out," Fred announced. "Use the trash cans on the way out, please. Let's keep it clean in here."

Jen Betters pulled Doug Savage aside for a quick interview as he headed for the door.

"Mr. Savage," she began, "what do you think of the verdict?"

"Well, I'm a little discouraged," Doug said. "I mean, I've worn this shirt with these pants before, and no one's ever told me—"

"Okay, that'll do," said Jen.

"—I shouldn't," Doug concluded.

"Thank you, Doug," Jen said hastily. "Here's Pip Peterson. How are you feeling?"

"Relieved," Pip answered with a smile, "and I'm looking forward to solving this condensation problem."

"Hmmm," Jen said. "Well, that's it from Science Court. I'm Jen Betters, and until the next time, the case is closed."

WHAT YOU NEED:

- two empty drinking glasses
- a freezer

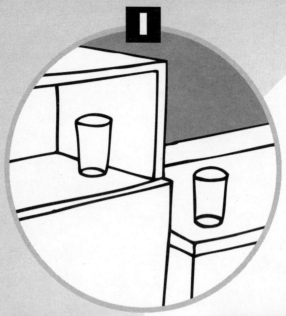

Put one empty glass in the freezer and let the other empty glass sit on a table or counter.

WHAT HAPPENS:

Water vapor from the air condenses on the outside of the cool glass.

2

After fifteen minutes, remove the glass from the freezer and place it next to the other one.

3

WHAT IT PROVES:

Water vapor does exist in the air. It changes to its liquid state when it comes in contact with a cool surface.

Observe both glasses. If the air is humid, you will see droplets of water form on the outside of the glass that was cooled in the freezer.

For more Science Court fun, and to find out how to bring Science Court into your classroom, visit our web site.
www.TeachTSP.com/classroom/SciCourt